Far far away, and further than t...
Lived a small, Mischievous Meerl...

With his extra long tail and 4 sharp claws. And his tiny dark brown button nose. Rings round his eyes And a small pointed face, Digging holes in the sand, all over the place.

And his sister and brother would run off scared, to shelter for cover, with one another.

But the meerkats grew to ignore these things,
Like "look there's an eagle flapping it's wings".

"An eagle an eagle coming in fast",
"It's not a prank, like I've done in the past".
"It's real it's coming, I swear it I say",
"Stop laughing and joking",
"Quick run away".

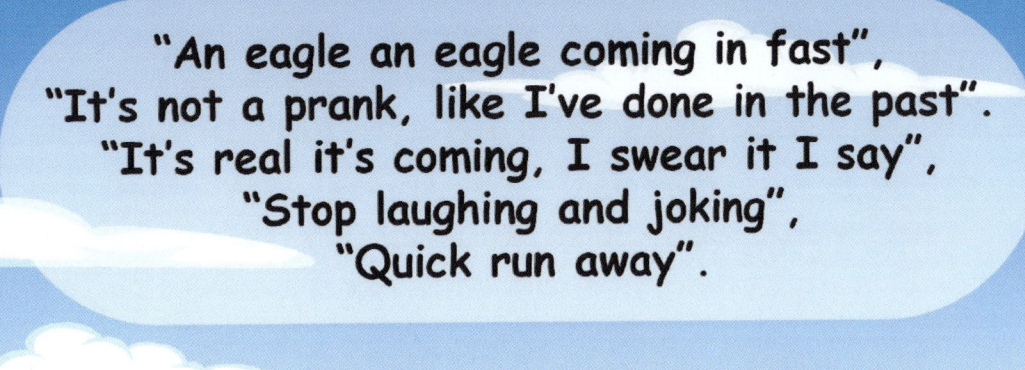

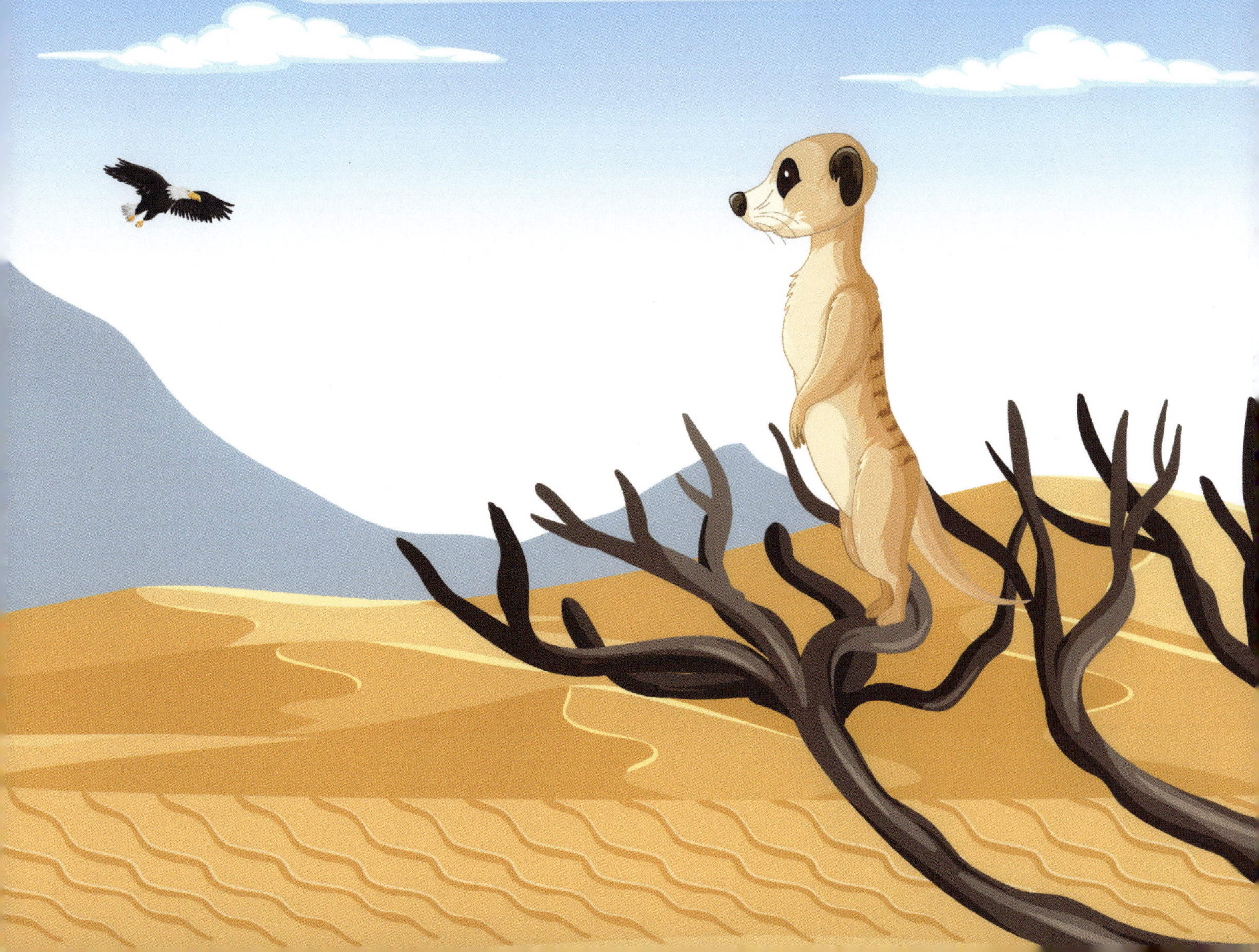

It missed the meerkats standing scared,
At the site of the big brown hungry bird
It grabbed the snake as it passed by,
And carried it away into the sky.

Printed in Great Britain
by Amazon

"Because if you lie about something untrue,
When it happens for real, people don't believe you".

An educational children's story about a Mischievous Little Meerkat that finds himself and his family in danger through his own actions.

Illustrated by: M.A Spari